Epinomis

A Modern Translation

Adapted for the Contemporary Reader

Plato

Translated by Tim Zengerink

Table of Contents

Preface - Message to the Reader

What If You Could Help Rebuild the Greatest Library in Human History?

Thousands of years ago, the Library of Alexandria stood as the crown jewel of human achievement — a sanctuary where the collected wisdom of every known civilization was gathered, preserved, and shared freely.

And then, it was lost.

Through fire, conquest, and the slow erosion of time, humanity lost not just books — but ideas, dreams, discoveries, and stories that could have changed the world forever.

Today, the Library of Alexandria lives again — and you are invited to be a part of its restoration.

Our mission is simple yet profound:

To rebuild the greatest library the world has ever known, and to translate all timeless works into every language and dialect, so that no seeker of knowledge is ever left behind again.

By joining our movement to rebuild the modern Library of Alexandria, you become part of an unprecedented mission:

- **Unlimited Access to the Greatest Audiobooks & eBooks Ever Written:**

  Instantly explore thousands of legendary works—Plato, Shakespeare, Jane Austen, Leo Tolstoy, and countless more. All instantly available to read or listen, placing a complete literary universe at your fingertips.

- **Beautiful Paperback & Deluxe Editions at Printing Cost**

  Own any title as an elegant paperback, deluxe hardcover, or stunning collectible boxset—offered to you at true printing cost, delivered straight to your door. Build your personal Library of Alexandria, crafted for beauty, built for durability, and worthy of proud display.

- **Fresh Translations for Modern Readers—in Every Language & Dialect**

  Enjoy timeless masterpieces reimagined in clear, contemporary language—no more outdated phrases or obscure references. Alongside the original versions, we're tirelessly translating these classics into every language and dialect imaginable, ensuring accessibility and understanding across cultures and generations.

- **Join a Global Renaissance of Literature & Knowledge**

  You directly support expanding our library, publishing deluxe editions at true cost, translating works into all global languages, and bringing humanity's greatest stories to people everywhere. By joining today, you're not just preserving a legacy of masterpieces; you set in motion a powerful wave of literary accessibility.

Become a Torchbearer of Knowledge.

Join us for free now at **LibraryofAlexandria.com**

Together, we will ensure that the light of human wisdom never fades again.

With gratitude and a shared love of knowledge,

The Modern Library of Alexandria Team

Visit:

www.libraryofalexandria.com

Or scan the code below:

Introduction

The Last Dialogue:
Between Plato's Legacy and
the Mysteries of the Stars

The Epinomis, often referred to as Plato's "fourteenth book of the Laws," is one of the most enigmatic works in the Platonic corpus. It emerges at the very edge of Plato's philosophical system, acting either as a summation of his late political theology or as an extension of it in an unexpected direction. While often excluded from collections of Plato's major dialogues due to questions of authorship—many scholars attribute it to Philip of Opus, a student and editor of Plato—the Epinomis remains a deeply significant and spiritually charged text. It offers readers a glimpse into the fusion of philosophy, religion, cosmology, and governance in what may be considered the final phase of the Platonic tradition.

The dialogue picks up where the Laws leaves off. In that dense and detailed legal and political treatise, Plato laid out a comprehensive system of governance meant to guide the ideal city—not as utopian as the Republic, but more practical and deeply grounded in religious reverence and civic discipline. The Epinomis, however, pushes this vision into even more metaphysical and mystical territory. It shifts focus from civic law to divine order, from the minutiae of legislation to the eternal movement of the stars and the soul's proper orientation toward the cosmos. It introduces a new ideal: the wise astronomer-priest, a ruler who understands not merely human law, but the divine structure of the universe itself.

At the heart of the Epinomis is a radical proposal: that true wisdom—the kind necessary for a well-ordered life and state—is not found in practical affairs or rhetorical skill, but in the study of divine astronomy. This astronomy is not the empirical science we know today, but a form of sacred contemplation that reveals the eternal truths of the gods and aligns the human soul with cosmic harmony. By learning to track the orderly revolutions of the heavens, the philosopher-priest is said to draw closer to the divine and thus becomes fit to govern both himself and others.

This move marks a notable shift in the Platonic trajectory. In earlier dialogues, knowledge of justice, the Good, and dialectical reasoning held primacy. Here, however, a kind of mystical piety grounded in celestial observation takes center stage. The Epinomis thus represents an important development in the synthesis of philosophy and theology—a development that would profoundly influence Neoplatonism and the esoteric traditions of Late Antiquity. Whether written by Plato himself or by his devoted student, the Epinomis serves as a spiritual capstone to the Platonic project, drawing the reader upward—from the city to the soul, and from the soul to the stars.

The dialogue's tone, structure, and terminology suggest that it was intended not as a public philosophical discourse, but as a more esoteric guide for those already initiated into the deepest layers of Platonic thought. As such, it is best read not simply as a philosophical argument, but as a spiritual invitation—one that calls the reader to a life of disciplined wonder, cosmological reverence, and divine law.

From Law to Cosmos:
The Evolution of the Platonic City

To grasp the Epinomis, one must first understand its relationship to the Laws. In the Laws, Plato moved away from the pure idealism of the Republic toward a more grounded and religious vision of the state. Here, the city is no longer ruled by philosopher-kings, but by carefully designed institutions, supported by myth, education, and a deeply ingrained reverence for the gods. The goal is to create not a perfect city, but a second-best city—one that fosters virtue, piety, and order among its citizens.

The Epinomis builds directly upon this foundation. However, it does not merely append a final thought to the legal blueprint. It transforms it. Where the Laws is preoccupied with civic education, social rituals, and the daily governance of the city, the Epinomis elevates the discussion to a cosmological plane. It argues that the ultimate aim of lawgiving is not merely social harmony, but divine alignment. A well-governed city is one in which the soul of each citizen is brought into accordance with the eternal rhythm of the heavens. Thus, astronomy—redefined as the contemplation of divine order—becomes the highest form of knowledge and the most sacred duty of rulers.

This is a startling pivot. In earlier works, Plato had emphasized mathematics, dialectic, and moral reasoning as the path to truth. The Epinomis, however, claims that true wisdom comes from an understanding of the motions of the celestial gods—the planets and stars. To be wise, one must be an astronomer. But this astronomy is not mechanical or mathematical; it is deeply theological. It sees the heavens as a living, divine order in which the gods reveal their will through perfect motion. To study the sky is to commune with the divine.

This idea links back to earlier Platonic themes. In the Timaeus, Plato introduced a vision of the cosmos as a living organism created by a divine craftsman. The Epinomis reaffirms and intensifies that vision. It positions the cosmos as the source of all law, all truth, and all morality. The state, then, must not only be just and orderly—it must be cosmically aligned. Its leaders must not only be educated in the laws, but in the eternal harmonies of the stars. Only then can the city mirror the order of the universe and nurture souls toward their divine destiny.

This cosmological turn also carries theological implications. The Epinomis insists that the greatest gods are not the anthropomorphic deities of popular religion, but the celestial beings—the sun, moon, planets, and stars—whose motions reflect eternal intelligence. This marks a shift from myth to cosmology, from narrative to law. It suggests a deeper, purer form of religion, one that demands intellectual discipline and philosophical reverence rather than sacrifice or superstition.

Theology, Education, and the Soul's Ascent

The Epinomis proposes a new model of education, one aimed not at producing skilled orators or obedient citizens, but at cultivating astronomer-priests—men who understand the divine order and live in accordance with it. This educational ideal combines rigorous study with spiritual devotion. It is both a philosophy and a way of life. Through disciplined contemplation of the heavens, the soul is purified, elevated, and prepared for a life of virtue and governance.

This education is not accessible to all. It is reserved for the few who are willing to undergo the intellectual and moral training required to grasp the eternal patterns of the cosmos. In this sense, the Epinomis aligns with the elitism found in much of Plato's work. It assumes that true wisdom is rare and that only a small class of guardians can rightly rule. But it also introduces a new religious dimension: the astronomer-priest is not only a ruler but a servant of the gods. His authority derives not from political power or dialectical prowess, but from his intimate understanding of divine law.

The soul, according to the Epinomis, finds its true fulfillment not in worldly success but in cosmic alignment. By learning the rhythms of the stars, the soul remembers its own divine origin and prepares for its return to the realm of eternal being. This is a form of philosophical mysticism—a belief that through knowledge, the soul can ascend, can become godlike, and can achieve immortality.

The text thus concludes not with a legal code, but with a cosmic vision. It affirms that the greatest good is not found in human affairs, but in divine contemplation. The ideal city, then, is a training ground for the soul, a place where laws and institutions serve as scaffolding for the ascent to higher knowledge and being. Politics becomes theology. Citizenship becomes discipleship. And the end of life is not social harmony, but spiritual union with the divine.

This vision would echo across centuries. The Epinomis profoundly influenced Neoplatonism, especially the works of Plotinus and Proclus, who saw in it a guide for the soul's ascent through the levels of reality. It also shaped early Christian thought, especially in its emphasis on celestial order, divine law, and the purification of the soul. In the Renaissance, it inspired mystics and scientists alike, from Marsilio Ficino to Johannes Kepler, who saw astronomy not just as a science but as a path to God.

In modern times, the Epinomis remains a challenging and provocative text. It confronts readers with a stark choice: to remain in the world of practical affairs or to turn upward, toward the eternal. It asks whether politics can ever be truly just without a foundation in divine truth, and whether knowledge can ever be complete without the vision of the whole.

For those who have journeyed through the Republic, the Timaeus, and the Laws, the Epinomis offers a final and mystical horizon. It is the threshold where philosophy becomes theology, where reason becomes reverence, and where the city dissolves into the stars. Whether read as Plato's last word or his disciple's tribute, it is a profound and enduring call to align life with the highest and most eternal truths.

Epinomis

Characters:
An Athenian Stranger,
Cleinias (a Cretan),
Megillus (a Lacedaemonian).

CLEINIAS:

As we agreed, the three of us—you, Megillus, and I—have gathered here to talk seriously about wisdom. We want to explore what it means for a person to use their mind in the best way possible, and how to live in a way that improves their soul. We've already talked about all the other parts of making laws and running a city. But we've left out the most important part—figuring out how a human being becomes truly wise. We haven't talked about that yet, and we haven't discovered the answer either. So let's not skip it now. If we do, we'll be missing the very point of this entire conversation—the reason we started this journey to begin with.

ATHENIAN:

You're right, Cleinias. But what I'm about to say might sound strange—and also not so strange. A lot of people, in both big cities and small towns, say the same thing: that human beings can never be completely blessed or happy. Now listen and decide for yourself if you think I'm saying something true.

I believe that it's almost impossible for people to be truly happy—at least while they're alive. Only a few people can even come close. But there's reason to hope that someone might find true happiness after death, especially if they lived a good and thoughtful life.

What I'm saying isn't some deep secret—it's something both Greeks and non-Greeks kind of already know. Every living creature starts life with difficulty. First comes the struggle of being conceived, then being born, and then growing up and getting educated. Every stage of life is full of challenges.

And even the short stretch of life we call adulthood—when things are supposed to be steady—is filled with problems. Then old age comes quickly, and most people wouldn't choose to live their life all over again unless they're naive or childish.

Now, how do I know this? Because even our search for wisdom shows it. We all seem to believe we can become wise. We chase after wisdom as if it's something our minds are naturally made to understand. But when we start studying the usual subjects—arts, sciences, skills—we quickly realize that none of them can really be called true wisdom.

Still, the soul feels confident, as if wisdom is something already inside it. But we can't seem to figure out exactly what it is or where it comes from. Doesn't that show how hard it is to truly understand wisdom?

Even so, there is hope—especially for those of us who are willing to examine ourselves carefully and discuss things with others using every kind of reasoning and conversation we can. So what do you think? Do we agree that this is how the search for wisdom really is?

CLEINIAS:

Yes, we agree, guest. And I hope that as time goes on, we'll figure out the truth with your help.

ATHENIAN:

Then the first thing we should do is look at all the other types of knowledge people usually study—what we call the sciences. But let's be clear: just having these skills doesn't make someone truly wise. So let's set them aside, one by one, so we can make room for the kind of knowledge we're actually missing—and then try to learn that instead.

Let's begin by looking at the kinds of knowledge humans need the most. These are the basic and most necessary ones. Even if someone becomes very skilled in these areas, people don't usually consider them wise—in fact, sometimes these skills bring more shame than praise. So, let's name these fields and show how most people who aim to be great avoid them, even though they require learning and thinking.

Take, for example, the skill that first led humans away from eating each other like wild animals and toward proper food. This was a major step forward. And while making flour and preparing food is good and useful, it doesn't make someone truly wise. Even working the land—farming—which seems natural to us, isn't really based on deep knowledge, but on instinct. Building houses, making tools, working with metals, crafting, and even trades like weaving and pottery— these are all helpful for everyday life, but they don't help us become virtuous or wise.

The same goes for hunting. It's clever, but not deeply wise. Even the arts of fortune-telling or interpreting signs don't lead to wisdom, because those who practice them know how to repeat what they've heard, but not whether it's true.

So we can say that although these useful skills help us survive, none of them lead to true wisdom. Next comes the world of the arts: imitation and performance.

People act, dance, paint, sing—they use tools and their own bodies to copy life in all kinds of ways. These are entertaining and beautiful, but they still don't teach us how to be wise. Then there's warfare—highly respected when needed, but mostly driven by courage and luck, not wisdom.

Medicine helps us deal with sickness caused by nature, but it, too, doesn't lead to deep wisdom. The same goes for sailors and pilots. They know their trade, but they don't understand the forces behind the winds and the sea. Lawyers and speakers, who know how to argue and impress in court, often fall short when it comes to true justice.

Now, there is a kind of skill that many people mistake for wisdom. When someone learns quickly, remembers well, and reacts cleverly, some say it's nature, some say it's wisdom. But anyone who truly understands will not call this real wisdom.

There must be a kind of knowledge that, when someone has it, they are wise for real, not just in name. Let's try to find that. Because we're looking for a form of understanding that goes beyond all the everyday skills—something that can really be called wisdom. And the person who has it will be neither silly nor simple, but truly wise and good. Whether this person is a leader or just a citizen, they will act justly and thoughtfully.

Let's consider the one type of knowledge that comes naturally to humans, and without which we would be the most ignorant of all creatures. It's not hard to figure out. It's the knowledge of numbers—of counting. I believe a god gave this gift to us, not by accident, but to help us survive. And I think it's fair to say that this god is the heavens—the sky, the stars, and everything above. It is just to honor it because it gives us everything good, including numbers, if we're willing to see it.

If someone watches the sky carefully—the stars moving, the seasons changing, the moon growing and shrinking—they will slowly learn to count: one, two, three, and so on. Even the slowest learner, given enough time watching day and night, will understand. The moon helps too. It grows bigger and smaller each month and shows a full cycle in about fifteen days. This teaches us to count the days, the months, and finally the year. Once we learn this, we can compare numbers to numbers and see patterns in nature.

And this knowledge of numbers connects to everything. It helps crops grow and guides the weather.

When things go wrong, it's not the heavens' fault, but ours—because we didn't live our lives fairly.

In our past conversations, we said that the things most helpful for people are easy to understand. Anyone can know what benefits us and what doesn't. Most things aren't too hard to figure out. But how to make people truly good? That's very hard.

It seems that we can get everything else—wealth, health, even success—without too much trouble. Everyone agrees we should take care of our bodies and souls. And everyone says we should be just, brave, and self-controlled. But when we ask what it means to be wise, or what wisdom really is, no one gives a clear answer.

Now, among all these ideas, we've found something new. It might not seem impressive at first, but it may be the key to wisdom. And if someone learns what we've just talked about, they might start to seem wise. But whether they are truly wise and good is something we still need to discuss.

CLEINIAS:

You've said something very thoughtful, guest. You're trying to speak seriously about important things.

ATHENIAN:

That's right, Cleinias. These topics aren't small matters. And even more challenging, they're completely true.

CLEINIAS:

Yes, they are. But don't let that stop you from saying what you mean.

ATHENIAN:

I won't. And I hope you'll be just as open to listening.

CLEINIAS:

I will. I'll speak for both of us when I say that.

ATHENIAN:

Good. Now, we need to start at the very beginning. First, let's try to see if we can describe wisdom with just one word. If we can't, we'll have to break it down and look at how many different skills or fields someone would need to learn to become wise.

CLEINIAS:

Go on.

ATHENIAN:

What I'm about to say should be acceptable for a lawmaker who tries to speak about the gods better and more respectfully than others before him. This person lives by good values, honors the gods, praises them with songs and prayers, and lives a good life.

CLEINIAS:

You're speaking well, guest. May your laws lead people to live pure lives, honor the gods, and end their lives in the best way.

ATHENIAN:

So how should we speak about this, Cleinias? Don't you think we show great respect to the gods by praising them and asking for the wisdom to speak well about them?

CLEINIAS:

Absolutely. Now, go ahead and offer your prayer, and say whatever you feel is the right thing about the gods.

ATHENIAN:

I will, if the gods lead me. You just pray along with me.

CLEINIAS:

Go ahead. Say what comes next.

ATHENIAN:

We need to start again from the beginning. Many past thinkers gave wrong ideas about how the gods and animals came into being. So now, based on what we said before, we need to give a better explanation. We should state clearly that gods do exist, that they care about everything, big or small, and that they can't be bribed by people who act unjustly. Do you remember this part, Cleinias? You even wrote it down because it was very true.

CLEINIAS:

Yes, I remember.

ATHENIAN:

Another thing we said is also important—that the soul is older than the body. Do you recall that? Or at least you remember that what is better, older, and more divine must come before what is worse, younger, and less noble. The one that leads must be older than what is led. So, we can agree that the soul comes before the body.

CLEINIAS:

Yes, I agree.

ATHENIAN:

If that's true, then the first thing created in the universe must have been something like a soul. So now we're getting close to understanding an important part of wisdom about how the gods came into being.

CLEINIAS:

Let's explain it as best we can.

ATHENIAN:

Let's begin by saying this: we can best describe a living creature as something that combines both soul and body to make one being.

CLEINIAS:

That sounds right.

ATHENIAN:

So a creature is rightly called an "animal" when body and soul are joined into one form.

CLEINIAS:

Yes.

ATHENIAN:

Now, let's consider the elements that were used to form the best and most beautiful things in the universe. There are five basic shapes or bodies. These are the building blocks of everything. Soul, which is the most divine, is invisible and capable of understanding, memory, and reasoning. It's the force that shapes and creates. Bodies, on the other hand, are visible and shaped by something else.

Let's name the five elements: fire, water, air, earth, and aether. Each of these creates its own kind of creature. Let's try to understand them one by one.

First, take everything that lives on the earth: humans, animals with many feet or none at all, those that move and those that stay in one place like plants. All of these come mostly from earth, though they include bits of the other elements too. Then we have another group of creatures that are mostly made of fire—these are visible creatures too.

Above these, in the heavens, there are other types of creatures—the stars. We should think of the stars as divine animals, made of beautiful bodies and excellent souls. We must think of them as either completely immortal or having such long lives that they don't need anything more. These star-beings are among the highest and most blessed kinds of creatures.

Let's start by remembering that, as we said before, there are two kinds of living things—one made mostly of fire, and the other of earth. Both kinds are visible. The earthy kind moves around in random ways, while the fiery kind moves in an orderly and regular way.

Now, things that move in a disorderly way usually don't have reason, like most of the creatures around us. But when something moves in a regular and ordered way, like the stars in the sky, that's a strong sign that it's intelligent. Their movement follows a steady and predictable pattern, which is proof that they act with purpose and thought.

Having a wise soul is the most important thing. A wise soul makes laws and leads, rather than being led. When such a soul acts with perfect reasoning, nothing can shake it—it becomes steady and unchanging, even more so than the hardest metal. According to the story, the three Fates (who control destiny) protect and carry out the plans of the gods in a perfect way.

So, if we want proof that the stars are intelligent beings, we can look at how they move. They always follow the same paths and do the same things over incredibly long periods of time. This shows their movements were carefully planned long ago and haven't changed. If their movements were random, changing up and down or in different patterns, that would show they lacked purpose. But it's the opposite—they move in the same, orderly way.

Most people get this backward. They think humans are intelligent because we move and change, but the stars are not intelligent because they stay in the same path. They think change means life and thought. But this isn't a good way to judge. In fact, it makes more sense to believe that what follows the same course over and over—what is steady and beautiful—is intelligent. The stars are like that. Their orderly, rhythmic dance in the sky provides what all creatures need.

If we want more evidence, just look at their size. The stars aren't small like they seem from earth. They're massive—far bigger than the Earth itself. Scientists and mathematicians can prove this. So, ask yourself: what kind of force or nature could make something that huge move perfectly and constantly forever? It must be something divine.

A god must be behind it all. Only a god could create living things, give them form, and move them in the best way possible. So, we can say with confidence: the Earth, the heavens, the stars, and everything else couldn't exist and work so precisely unless a soul lived in them or guided them. Without a soul, none of this would hold together.

So, people shouldn't talk carelessly about these things. If someone claims that random forces or blind nature caused all this order, they're not saying anything meaningful.

Let's go back and think carefully. We said that two main things exist: soul and body. Everything else comes from them. They are totally different from each other. The soul is intelligent and rules; the body is not intelligent and is ruled. The soul causes things to happen; the body just experiences them. So, saying that the stars or the sky were made by anything other than soul and body doesn't make sense.

If we want to be clear and consistent, we must either say the stars themselves are gods or say they were made by gods as divine images. Either way, they deserve honor above all statues. No statue humans have made is more beautiful, more lasting, or placed in more perfect positions than the stars.

So, let's agree that there are two main kinds of visible living beings: one kind is immortal (like the stars), and the other is mortal and comes from the earth (like us). There are also three other kinds in between these two. First after fire comes aether, from which the soul shapes some animals that are mostly made from aether, but also a little from other elements to hold them together. After that, soul creates animals from air, and then from water.

It's likely that the soul used all five elements to create every kind of life it could, filling the entire universe with living beings. These creations begin with the gods that we can see and end with humans like us.

As for the gods—Zeus, Hera, and the others—let everyone place them where they think best, as long as they follow the same reasoning we've used here.

Let's start by recognizing that the stars and the things that move with them are visible gods. They are the greatest, most deserving of honor, and they see everything clearly from all sides. They should be ranked first. Right after them, in second place, come the spirits or "daemons." These are unseen beings made of air who move quietly between heaven and earth. They help deliver messages between gods and humans. Even though we can't see them clearly, they are nearby. They're smart, have good memories, and understand our thoughts. They love good, honest people and dislike the wicked.

The true gods, the ones beyond pain and pleasure, think and understand everything. The sky is filled with life, and these beings in the middle carry messages quickly throughout heaven and earth. Some other beings, formed from water, are like demigods. Sometimes they're visible, sometimes not. When they do appear, they're mysterious and hard to understand.

There are five kinds of living beings in total. We might meet them in dreams, visions, or signs at important moments in life—like during illness, death, or sacred ceremonies. Because of this, a wise lawmaker should never carelessly change the religion of the city. He shouldn't reject or replace any part of his country's beliefs about the gods, especially if he doesn't know what he's doing. Human nature just isn't made to fully understand the divine.

It's just as wrong when someone refuses to honor the real gods and instead treats them like they don't matter. That's like someone who sees the Sun and Moon shining above us and yet refuses to speak of them with respect, ignoring the need to celebrate them with festivals or prayers. If someone acted like that, we'd rightly say they're doing harm to themselves and others.

CLEINIAS: Of course—we'd say that person is one of the worst.

ATHENIAN: Then know this, Cleinias. This exact mistake almost happened to me.

CLEINIAS: What do you mean?

ATHENIAN: I've seen eight great celestial powers moving in the sky, like siblings. But I didn't do much about it—although anyone could observe what I did. Three of them I've already mentioned: the Sun, the

Moon, and the fixed stars. But there are five more. We shouldn't think some of them are gods while others aren't. They're all siblings and deserve equal honor. We shouldn't celebrate one every year and another every month, or assign some to different times just because of their paths. They all move in patterns that reason—the most divine force—has made visible to us.

A wise and fortunate person will be drawn to learn from these patterns. That person will live well and, after death, reach a place fit for the soul. Someone who truly learns and lives wisely will enjoy the most beautiful things as a reward, in both life and afterlife.

Now let's talk about the eight heavenly bodies I mentioned. I've already named three. The fourth and fifth move at nearly the same speed as the Sun. They are probably Venus and Mercury. These two move closely with the Sun and are guided by divine reason. One of them doesn't have a common name because the person who first noticed it was a foreigner. Long ago, people in Egypt and Syria were the first to study the stars, since their clear skies gave them a perfect view of the heavens. Their ideas have spread to us over thousands of years. That's why we can confidently say these things should become part of our laws.

It would be foolish not to honor these divine bodies. The reason they don't have names for most people is because those names come from foreign languages. For example, the star called both Morning Star and Evening Star (Venus) was named by a Syrian. Mercury, which moves with the Sun, also got its name this way.

There are three stars that move with the Sun and Moon toward the right in the sky. The eighth, outermost circle moves in the opposite direction, and it pulls the others along. That might seem strange to people who aren't trained in astronomy, but those who know better can see the truth. Real wisdom reveals itself to anyone who has even a small bit of divine understanding.

Three stars remain to be named. One moves very slowly and is called Phaenon—what we know as Saturn. The next one, moving a little faster, is Phaethon— Jupiter. The third, and fastest of these, is Puroeis— Mars—which is known for its red color. These things are not hard to describe. But once learned, they should be remembered and understood, just as we've explained.

We should all remember this: we Greeks live in one of the best places for developing good character. The land we live in is balanced—not too hot, not too cold— and it helps us think clearly about the gods and the universe. Even if the Barbarians had certain ideas first, the Greeks often take those same ideas and improve them, making them clearer and more beautiful. And that includes how we think about the gods.

It's hard to understand everything about the gods without some doubt, but we can still hope that the Greeks, with their traditions, teachings, and oracles like the one at Delphi, will show more respect for the gods in better ways than others have before. No Greek should think it's wrong to try to understand the gods. The gods are wise, not ignorant. They know that people can learn, and that they can learn about the gods too. If the gods didn't know this, they'd be foolish—like not even knowing themselves. But clearly, they do teach us, and we do learn.

It's also important to think about how people first began to understand the gods. In the beginning, people may have thought about fire, water, and other natural things as being the oldest forces in the world. But later, they began to think about the soul—a more amazing thing. Some believed the body could move and act through heat and cold, but that the soul couldn't move itself. Now we say that the soul does move the body and itself, and that it's no surprise if the soul can guide motion. In fact, the soul causes everything in the universe. Good souls lead toward good things, and bad souls lead toward bad. The good soul must win over the bad ones.

All of this helps explain Justice—a force that punishes the wicked and rewards the good. And it shows that people who are truly good must also be wise.

Let's now return to the kind of wisdom we were trying to find earlier. Can we reach it through learning or training? Is there some knowledge that, without it, we would remain ignorant of justice and virtue?

I think so. And now I'll try to explain it in a way that I myself understand clearly. A big part of virtue, if used the wrong way, can actually lead to ignorance. But we must not believe anyone who says there's something more important to humans than piety—respect for the gods. True piety doesn't come from ignorance. The best kind of people are hard to find, but when they do exist and receive the right education, they can become a blessing to others. They are calm, brave, smart, good at learning, and love knowledge.

When raised the right way, these people can teach the rest of society the right things to do and say about the gods—what to sacrifice, when to purify, and how to worship. They don't pretend to be good with fake appearances; they are truly virtuous. This part of life is the most important for any society. If there is a teacher for it, it can be learned beautifully and properly. But no one can teach it unless the gods help. And even if someone teaches it the wrong way, it's better not to learn it at all than to learn it badly.

So, I say again: this kind of nature is the best. Let's now try to understand how someone could learn these things—about god-worship—by explaining it in a way that fits both the speaker and the listener.

It may sound strange, but the subject we need to learn is called astronomy. Not the kind of astronomy that looks at when stars rise and set, like Hesiod talks about. I mean the kind that studies the orbits of the eight spheres—the seven lower ones, and the one highest of all. This is not easy. Only people with special natures can understand it. But we can still teach the right people the right way to learn.

Start with the Moon. It moves the fastest and marks the months and full moons. Next is the Sun, which controls the seasons. Then come the other orbits, which are harder to understand. To learn all of this, students need a solid background—especially in mathematics.

First comes the study of numbers—not just numbers used for measuring objects, but pure numbers. From this, we move on to geometry. Geometry shows how numbers relate to shapes. It reveals patterns that are not just human but divine.

After geometry comes the study of solid shapes and space—what experts call stereometry. This, too, is amazing and divine. All of nature seems to follow the pattern of numbers and ratios. There's a kind of music and rhythm built into the universe. Even music itself is based on number and proportion.

All of this helps lead to a better understanding of the visible universe. If someone hasn't studied these subjects, they won't really be able to grasp the divine order of things. We must also learn to ask the right questions and test wrong ideas. This is the best way to reach the truth.

We should also study time carefully—how exactly it keeps everything in order in the heavens. If we believe the soul is older and more divine than the body, then we should also believe that everything is full of gods, and that the gods are never careless or forgetful of us.

If someone understands all this, it brings great benefits. If not, they should at least keep praying to the gods with respect. The method for learning is this: anyone who wants to learn properly must understand diagrams, numbers, musical harmony, and the way all the stars move in agreement. All of this can be seen as one connected system. Without this kind of learning, no person or state will ever truly thrive.

This is the way—the right training. And it must be followed, whether it's easy or not. We must not ignore the gods. The path has been made clear. And I call the person who understands this truly wise. I say it seriously: when such a person dies, having learned and lived this way, they will be blessed. Whether they lived on the mainland or an island, in public or in private life, their soul will be fortunate, wise, and happy.

And just as we said at the beginning, it still holds true: only a few people can ever be completely happy and blessed. And we are right to say this. For only those who are truly good, naturally gifted, and well-educated in the ways we've just described will receive the best of life's rewards.

To those who've lived this way, we say both in private and public law: the highest honors and greatest positions should go to the elders who've achieved this kind of wisdom. The rest should follow their lead and praise the gods with devotion.

Finally, we should all, after understanding and reflecting on this wisdom, join together in honoring it through the sacred gathering called the "nocturnal assembly."

The End

Thank You for Reading

Dear Reader,

We hope this timeless classic has sparked your imagination and enriched your literary journey. Now that you've turned the final page, we want to share a vision for the future of reading—one where every classic you've ever wanted to explore is at your fingertips, in a format that best suits your life.

We'd like to invite you to gain immediate, unlimited digital & audiobook access to hundreds of the most treasured literary classics ever written—along with the option to secure deluxe paperback, hardcover & box set editions at printing cost. Together, we can spark a new global literary renaissance alongside our small, independent publishing house called "The Library of Alexandria."

Thousands of years ago, the Library of Alexandria stood as a beacon of knowledge—until it was lost to history. We aim to reignite that spirit of preservation and discovery right now, in the modern age—only this time, it's accessible to all, in every language and every format.

Picture a world where every timeless classic, novel, poem, or philosophical treatise is not only available to read but also updated for today's readers—modernized, translated into any language or dialect, and ready to enjoy in any format you choose, whether that is in an eBook, audiobook, paperback, or deluxe hardcover & box set version a printing cost.

By joining our movement to rebuild the modern Library of Alexandria, you become part of an unprecedented mission to offer:

- **Unlimited Audiobook & eBook Access to the Greatest Classics of All Time**

  Instantly explore thousands of legendary works, from Plato and Shakespeare to Jane Austen and Leo Tolstoy. All are instantly ready to read or listen to, giving you a complete literary universe at your fingertips.

- **Paperback & Deluxe Editions at Printing Costs:**

  Purchase any title in a paperback, deluxe hardbound, or deluxe boxset edition at printing costs, shipped right to your doorstep. Curate your personal library of Alexandria with editions worthy of display— crafted to last, designed to captivate, and delivered straight to your door.

- **Modern translations for Contemporary Readers in all languages and dialects**

  Discover a vast selection of classics reimagined in clear, current language—no more struggling with outdated phrases or obscure references. Next to the original versions, we aim to offer translations in as many languages and dialects as possible.

  As we continue our translation efforts and add new languages, readers everywhere can connect with these works as if they were written today. By bridging linguistic divides, you're contributing to ensuring that these timeless stories become more meaningful, accessible, and inspiring for people across the globe.

- **Your Personal Library of Alexandria:**

  Over the months and years, you'll curate a unique physical archive of classics—each volume a testament to your taste, curiosity, and love of knowledge. It's not just about owning books—it's about curating a cultural legacy you'll cherish and pass down for generations to come.

- **Join a Global Literary Renaissance:**

  Your support fuels an ongoing mission: allowing us to reinvest in offering deluxe print editions (including special boxsets) at their true cost, broaden the range of available formats and translations, and extend the reach of these works to new audiences worldwide. By joining today, you're not just preserving a legacy of masterpieces; you set in motion a powerful wave of literary accessibility.

We are more than a publisher—we're a movement, and we can't do it alone. Your support lets us scale our mission, preserving and reimagining history's greatest works for tomorrow's readers.

Become a Torchbearer of knowledge.

Thank you for picking up this book and allowing us into your literary journey. As you turn the pages, know that you're part of something larger: a global effort to keep these stories alive, share their wisdom across borders and generations, and spark a true cultural revival for the modern era.

If this resonates with you—please consider taking the next step by visiting:

www.libraryofalexandria.com

With gratitude and a shared love of knowledge,

The Modern Library of Alexandria Team

Visit:

www.libraryofalexandria.com

Or scan the code below: